Lane Roberts Presents...

Could A Dog Be President?

Illustrated by Dodot Asmoro

For all you mutt lovers.

If you asked either one
     how long they'd been friends,
both would reply that they
     could not remember when
the day Wendy met the mutt,
     which brightens her world,
just seems she'd always known
     her dear Katy Girl.

At the end of each day,
     they'd snuggle in a heap.
Wendy loved that Katy Girl
     would grunt in her sleep.
Each day they found something
     more fun than their toys.
But, helping other people
     was what they enjoyed.

Like, when Mr. Boots was gardening,
     and lost his rake,
Wendy lent him hers
     while Katy searched near the lake.
And then, Patti lived next door
     was somewhat home-bound.
The girls helped out
     with all her chores to nail down.

Then, Kristi who cried
     when her family sold the farm,
leaned on Wendy's shoulder
     while Katy nuzzled her arm.
Yes, the girls were always
     an inseparable pair.
Helping out others
     was how they showed that they cared.

That night at dinner,
      Wendy's parents in a huff,
discussing elections
      and other grown up stuff.
"We want a true leader",
      Wendy's mother would say.
Her father then agreed
      with more thoughts he conveyed.

"Someone who helps others
      is really what we need.
Not someone simply hungry
      for power and greed."
It was like a tennis match
      of comments and nerves.
Her father returned statements
      while mother would serve.

In bed while snuggling,
    and Katy grunting away,
Wendy thought about the verbal
    game her folks played.
She froze for a moment,
    an idea on the verge.
Her body lit with joy
    when it finally emerged.

"That's it!", Wendy cried,
    "problems are always unclogged.
Don't vote for a person,
    but elect us a DOG!!!"
And grunting beside her,
    the best mutt for the part.
How could they lose,
    if the girls followed their heart?

Elections are easy
        you just count up the votes,
and the winner's the one
        who has gotten the most.
There'd be three days of voting
        to see who would win.
The girls needed more than just
        the votes from their friends.

So, Wendy first approached
        her neighbor Mr, Clump,
known to be standoffish
        and a bit of a grump.
Wendy shared her idea.
        Mr. Clump asked and huffed,
"Can a dog be president?",
        the challenge seemed tough.

Mr. Clump said his decision
        was now quite sound.
There's no way in the world
        that he'd vote for a hound.
Another person was running
        Clump said he'd choose.
If the girls weren't creative,
        they likely would lose.

On the first voting day,
        things seemed kind of scary,
until they met animals,
        at the sanctuary.
They spoke with apes and giraffes
        about their intent,
and of course they asked,
        "Can a dog be president"?

Then suddenly a shriek,
        a lion mother cried.
It seems that her cub
        had gotten lost from the pride.
The animals scattered
        and were searching around.
Katy Girl, instantly,
        put her nose to the ground.

She picked up the cub's scent
     and was sniffing about,
investigating scenes
     with the tip of her snout.
Within minutes, she pointed
     to an old tree fort.
Wendy climbed the branches
     with a thankful report.

The frightened cub now safe
     by the lioness's side
convinced all the critters
     Katy's most qualified
to serve as their leader
     in this president's race.
The first day of voting
     Katy landed third place.

On the second day, the girls
      rode bikes to a farm.
Wendy knew Katy Girl
      had a natural charm.
They spoke to animals,
      and to greater extent,
they also wondered,
      "Could a Dog Be President"?

Farmer interrupted, shouting,
      "NO TIME TO WASTE!".
His entire herd of cattle
      had broken down the gate.
Animals were scurrying,
      and all were alarmed,
everyone was in danger
      of a stampede through the farm.

Quicker than an eye blink,
    Katy Girl was away,
heading towards the cattle
    she knew how to persuade,
back to their old pasture,
    where green grass grows thick.
Katy Girl's herding skills
    were just an old dog's trick.

All the animals were impressed,
    from the pigs to the ducks,
who voted for Katy Girl,
    giving her all of their luck.
The second day of voting,
    she moved up a spot,
Katy Girl now stood in
    second place from the top.

There's one animal group
        the girls needed to reach.
On the final day, they rode
        their bikes to the beach.
The dolphins began asking,
        in any event,
Is it possible "Could,
        a Dog be President"?

Nearby, Wendy noticed
        turtles rushing for land.
Apparently a shark,
        was somewhere close at hand.
But, Katy had quickly
        jumped into a canoe,
paddling towards turtles,
        she's determined to rescue.

She protected turtles
        from angry, hungry sharks.
Any fish wanting them
        must face a Katy bark.
Thankful turtles asked,
        if they could use Katy's boat,
heading off with dolphins
        to finally cast their vote.

Near the end of the day,
     she was tied for the lead.
Only one vote was left
     to decide who'd succeed.
Turns out it's Mr. Clump's,
     the grumpy neighbor gent,
who said he'd never vote
     for a dog as President.

Others who're running,
     tried to get Clump to choose them,
throwing him promises,
     pretending he's a friend.
Never seeing a woman
     who tripped on the street.
Clump saw the girls help
     and his heart then skipped a beat.

Clump knew he'd never seen
     someone quite as kind.
Was seeing the girls help
     enough to change his mind?
He left to cast his vote
     and was feeling quite content.
Whomever Clump would choose,
     would be our President.

Clump chose Katy Girl
    who would lead the country now.
Because, she cares for all
    from humans to the cows.
People celebrated,
    and Clump who helped them through,
was chased by reporters
    who want an interview.

Parades, fireworks,
    and a calmness through the land.
A leader cared for folks
    who seemed to understand,
being a great president,
    is not just a claim,
but **helping everyone**,
    should be your greatest aim.

As they close their sleepy eyes,
    the world changed that night.
A girl and her Katy dog
    inspired what was right.
Others began looking
    at problems to confront,
while Wendy fell asleep
    to the sound of Katy grunts.

ABOUT THE PROJECT - the author, the illustrator, the...2nd assistant to the typist.

Conceived in fun, and dedicated to the proposition that sharing stories connects us to one another, Lane has been marinating ideas for this story since the success of his first book, "Ryan Runs With The Black Wolf Bear". Departing from the more reflective experience of that book, "Could A Dog Be President" characterizes Lane's natural playfulness. One challenge in its creation was the delicate tiptoeing through the sometimes absurd nature of American politics. But, since Lane self-proclaims many of his own ideas to also be quite "absurd", marrying these two concepts naturally generated a creative seed. Once that seed is firmly planted, he feels an artistic compulsion to care for the crop until it blooms. Since Lane also loves the natural comedy that emulates from anthropomorphization, this spirit easily made its way into the story.

The real challenge with the project was locating an illustrator who shared in Lane's natural silliness and goofey sense of humor. Once more, that energy also needed to find it's way onto the page. Through the advisement of several fantastic contributing illustrators, including: Florina Baldi, Sabuj Art Neon Green, and Milan Designs, Lane finally settled on Dodot Asmoro as his running mate. A graduate of Visual Communication Design Faculty Institute of Art, Dodot has won many design competitions as an illustrator and animator. Having illustrated many children's books, Dodot loves drawing kids, comics, animals, and nature. His use of a wide range of colors enhances his funny and witty drawings, and it is clear he has a passion for art.

Dodot lives in Jakarta, Indonesia and can be found online at Instagram @dodotasmoro or via Facebook – Dodot Asmoro.

Lane lives, writes, and breathes in Chicago, and can be found through virtually any social media outlet @writtenbylane or at www.writtenbylane.com.

Published in the United States of America by Lane Roberts.

ISBN-13: 978-0-578-74403-2 (Lane Roberts)

BISAC: Juvenile Fiction / Pets

First Edition

Made in the USA
Monee, IL
02 October 2021